# THE BARNYARD SONG

Retold by STEVEN ANDERSON

Illustrated by DAN TAYLOR

CANTATA
LEARNING

MANKATO, MINNESOTA

WWW.CANTATALEARNING.COM

Washington County Public Library
205 Oak Hill Street
Abingdon, VA 24210

**CANTATA**
**LEARNING**
MANKATO, MINNESOTA

Published by Cantata Learning
1710 Roe Crest Drive
North Mankato, MN 56003
www.cantatalearning.com

Library of Congress Control Number: 2014957030
978-1-63290-286-3 (hardcover/CD)
978-1-63290-438-6 (paperback/CD)
978-1-63290-480-5 (paperback)

*The Barnyard Song* by Steven Anderson
Illustrated by Dan Taylor

Book design, Tim Palin Creative
Editorial direction, Flat Sole Studio
Executive musical production and direction, Elizabeth Draper
Music arranged and produced by Steven C Music

Printed in the United States of America.

VISIT

**WWW.CANTATALEARNING.COM/ACCESS-OUR-MUSIC**

TO SING ALONG TO THE SONG

When animals talk, what do they say?

Sing this song to find out!

I had a cat, and my cat **pleased** me.
I fed my cat under **yonder** tree.
And my cat says, "Fiddle-eye-fee!"

7

I had a duck, and my duck pleased me.
I fed my duck under yonder tree.
And my duck says, "Quack, quack!"
And my cat says, "Fiddle-eye-fee!"

Quack,
quack!

I had a goose, and my goose pleased me.
I fed my goose under yonder tree.

"Quaw, quaw!"

"Quack! quack!"

"Fiddle-ee-ee!"

12

And my goose says, "Quaw, quaw!"
And my duck says, "Quack, quack, quack!"
And my cat says, "Fiddle-eye-fee!"

I had a cow, and my cow pleased me.

I fed my cow under yonder tree.

And my cow says, "Moo, moo!"
And my goose says, "Quaw, quaw!"
And my duck says, "Quack, quack!
And my cat says, "Fiddle-eye-fee!"

I had a horse, and my horse pleased me.

I fed my horse under yonder tree.

And my horse says, "Neigh, neigh!"
And my cow says, "Moo, moo!"
And my goose says, "Quaw, quaw!"
And my duck says, "Quack, quack!"
And my cat says, "Fiddle-eye-fee!

Quaw! quaw!

Neigh, neigh!

Moo, moo!

Fiddle-eye-fee!

Quack, quack!

# SONG LYRICS
## The Barnyard Song

I had a cat, and my cat pleased me.
I fed my cat under yonder tree.
And my cat says, "Fiddle-eye-fee!"

I had a duck, and my duck pleased me.
I fed my duck under yonder tree.
And my duck says, "Quack, quack!"
And my cat says, "Fiddle-eye-fee!"
I had a goose, and my goose pleased
    me.
I fed my goose under yonder tree.

And my goose says, "Quaw, quaw!"
And my duck says, "Quack, quack!"
And my cat says, "Fiddle-eye-fee!"

I had a cow, and my cow pleased me.
I fed my cow under yonder tree.

And my cow says, "Moo, moo!"
And my goose says, "Quaw, quaw!"
And my duck says, "Quack, quack!
And my cat says, "Fiddle-eye-fee!"

I had a horse, and my horse pleased
    me.
I fed my horse under yonder tree.

And my horse says, "Neigh, neigh!"
And my cow says, "Moo, moo!"
And my goose says, "Quaw, quaw!"
And my duck says, "Quack, quack!"
And my cat says, "Fiddle-eye-fee!

# The Barnyard Song

Americana
Steven C Music

### Verses 3-5

**Verse 4**
I had a cow, and my cow pleased me.
I fed my cow under yonder tree,
And my cow says, "Moo, moo!"
And my goose says, "Quaw, quaw!"
And my duck says, "Quack, quack!"
And my cat says, "Fiddle-eye-fee!"

(Instrumental)

**Verse 5**
I had a horse, and my horse pleased me.
I fed my horse under yonder tree,
And my horse says, "Neigh, neigh!"
And my cow says, "Moo, moo!"
And my goose says, "Quaw, quaw!"
And my duck says, "Quack, quack!"
And my cat says, "Fiddle-eye-fee!"

# GLOSSARY

**pleased**—to be made happy or glad

**yonder**—over there

# GUIDED READING ACTIVITIES

1. Draw or list all of the characters, people, and animals in this story. What noise does each one make?

2. Add two more animals to the story. What sounds do those animals make?

3. Look back at one of the illustrations. Tell a story about what is happening in the illustration.

## TO LEARN MORE

Dickman, Nancy. *Farm Animals*. Chicago: Raintree, 2011.

Hernandez, Christopher. *Animals on the Farm*. New York: Cartwheel Books, 2012.

Rissman, Rebecca. *Animals*. Chicago: Raintree, 2013.

Van Fleet, Matthew. *Moo*. New York: Simon & Schuster, 2011.